The Tempest

Sweet Cherry

Published by Sweet Cherry Publishing Limited
Unit 36, Vulcan House,
Vulcan Road,
Leicester, LE5 3EF
United Kingdom

First published in the UK in 2012
2020 edition

4 6 8 10 9 7 5 3

ISBN: 978-1-78226-014-1

© Macaw Books

The Tempest

Based on the original story by William Shakespeare,
adapted by Macaw Books.

Lexile® code numerical measure L = Lexile® 1070L

Guided Reading Level = T

Cover design and illustrations by Macaw Books

www.sweetcherrypublishing.com

Printed and bound in China
C.GD.012

About Shakespeare

William Shakespeare, regarded as the greatest writer in the English language, was born in Stratford-upon-Avon in Warwickshire, England (around 23 April 1564). He was the third of eight children born to John and Mary Shakespeare.

Shakespeare was a poet, playwright and dramatist. He is often known as England's national poet and the 'Bard of Avon'. Thirty-eight plays, one hundred and fifty-four sonnets, two long narrative poems and several other poems are attributed to him. Shakespeare's plays have been translated into every major existent language and are performed more often than those of any other playwright.

Prospero: He is the play's protagonist. He was the Duke of Milan until his brother plotted against him and usurped him. He has spent twelve years on an island.

Miranda: She is Prospero's daughter. She is compassionate, loyal to her father and non-judgmental.

Ferdinand:
He is the son
of the King of
Naples. He falls
in love with
Miranda when
he first sees her
and is just as
naive as her.

Ariel: He is a supernatural being, a spirit. He is mischievous, powerful and does all that Prospero asks of him.

The Tempest

Prospero, the Duke of Milan, was a learned man, who lived among his books, leaving the management of his dukedom to his brother, Antonio, in whom

he had complete trust. But Antonio wanted to become the duke himself, and plotted his brother's death. With the help of Prospero's enemy, Alonso, the King of Naples, Antonio managed to get what he wanted. They took Prospero to sea, and when they were far away from land, forced him into a little boat with no tackle, mast or sail. They put his little daughter, Miranda (not yet three years old), into the boat with

him and sailed away, leaving them to their fate. So, in this treacherous manner, Antonio usurped the dukedom of Milan.

But one among the courtiers, Lord Gonzalo, was true to his rightful master, Prospero. He secretly placed some fresh

water, provisions and clothes
in the boat, along with what
Prospero valued most of all –
some of his precious books. After
a rough ride at sea for several
days, the boat finally reached an
island, and Prospero and his little
daughter disembarked safely.

12

This island was enchanted. For years it had been under the spell of a wicked witch, Sycorax, who had imprisoned all the good spirits in the trunks of trees. She died shortly before Prospero was cast on the shores, but the spirits, the chief of whom was called Ariel, still remained imprisoned.

Now, Prospero was a great magician. He had devoted himself to the study of magic over the years while his brother had managed the affairs of Milan. By using his magic

he set free the imprisoned spirits,
yet kept them obedient to his
will. Prospero treated them
kindly as long as they did his
bidding, and exercised his
power over them wisely.

There was one creature, though, whom Prospero found it necessary to treat with harshness – this was Caliban, the son of the wicked witch. He was

a hideous, deformed monster,
vicious and brutal in nature.
Caliban, whom Prospero taught
to speak, did not want to learn
anything good or useful and was
therefore employed as a slave
to fetch wood and do all the

laborious work; and Ariel had
the responsibility of compelling
him to do these services. The
lively little Ariel had nothing
mischievous in his nature,
except that he took pleasure
in tormenting Caliban. When

18

Caliban was lazy and neglected his work, Ariel (who was invisible to all except Prospero) would pinch him, and sometimes make him trip up and fall over.

Having the powerful spirits, both good and bad, obedient to

his will, Prospero could by their
means command the winds,
and the waves of the sea.

Miranda grew up into a
young girl, sweet and fair. Once,
it so happened that Antonio
and Alonso, with Sebastian,

Alonso's brother, and Ferdinand,
Alonso's son, were at sea
together with Lord Gonzalo,
and their ship came near
Prospero's island. Seeing this,
Prospero gave orders to the
spirits to raise a violent storm.

While the tempest was raging, Prospero showed his daughter the big ship trying to fight the waves, and told her that it was filled with living human beings like themselves. Miranda, feeling sad for them, requested that her father stop what he was doing. Prospero told her that he intended to save

every one of them. Then, for the first time, he told her the story of his life, and that he had caused this storm to rise so that his enemies, Antonio and Alonso, who were on-board, would be delivered into his hands.

Ending the story, Prospero gently touched his daughter with his magic wand and she fell fast asleep. Ariel, the spirit, had just

then presented himself before his master to give an account of the tempest. The spirits were always invisible to Miranda, but even so, Prospero did not like to talk to them in his daughter's presence.

Ariel described the storm and how the king's son, Ferdinand, had been the first to leap into the sea, and how his father thought his dear son had been swallowed

27

up by the waves. "But he is safe,"
said Ariel, "in a corner of the
island, sitting sadly, lamenting
the loss of his father, who he
assumes to be drowned."

"Where are the king and
my brother?" asked Prospero.

"I left them searching for Ferdinand," answered Ariel. "Of the ship's crew no one is missing; though each one thinks himself to be the only one saved. And the ship is safe in the harbour."

"Well done, Ariel, but there is more work to be done yet," said Prospero. "Now bring the young prince here. My daughter must see him."

"More work?" exclaimed Ariel. "Let me remind you, master, you have promised me my freedom."

"I remember all," said Prospero. "But you

do not seem to recollect what torment I freed you from. Have you forgotten how the wicked witch Sycorax imprisoned you in a tree?"

"Pardon me, dear master," said Ariel, ashamed at having appeared ungrateful; "I will obey your commands."

"Do so," said Prospero, "and I will set you free."

Away went Ariel, taking the form of a water nymph, to where he had left Ferdinand. Invisible to him, Ariel hovered nearby and began singing.

"Full fathom five thy father lies;
Of his bones are coral made.
Those are pearls that were his eyes;
Nothing of him that doth fade.
But doth suffer a sea-change;
Into something rich and strange.
Sea-nymphs hourly ring his knell.

Hark! Now I hear them, ding dong bell!"

The news of his lost father soon roused the prince and made him follow the sound of Ariel's voice until it led him to Prospero and Miranda, who were sitting in the shade of a large tree.

Then, everything happened as Prospero desired. Miranda, who had not seen any other human being except her father for as long as she could

remember, looked at the youthful
prince with wonder in her eyes
and love in her heart. Ferdinand,
seeing such a lovely girl in this
deserted place, and after hearing
the strange song, thought he
was on an enchanted island and
that Miranda was its goddess.

But Prospero, though
secretly delighted, pretended

to be angry. "You have come here as a spy," he shouted at Ferdinand. "I will chain your neck and feet together, and you shall feed on freshwater mussels and withered roots, and have seawater to drink. Follow me."

"No," said Ferdinand, and drew his sword. But Prospero,

41

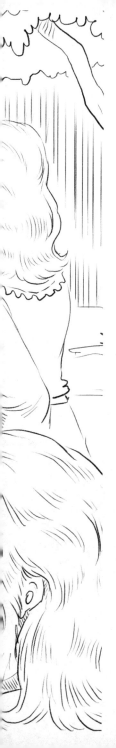

waving his magic
wand, fixed him to
the spot so that he
stood as still as a
stone statue. In terror,
Miranda requested that
her father have mercy
on the young prince,
but Prospero refused
to do so and made
Ferdinand follow him
to his cell. There he
made the prince work
hard, carrying heavy
logs of timber and piling
them up. Ferdinand
patiently obeyed.

Miranda offered
to help Ferdinand, but

he refused; yet he could not keep from her the secret of his love, and she, upon hearing it, rejoiced and promised to be his wife. Hearing them profess their love for each other, Prospero released Ferdinand from his servitude and, glad at heart, gave his consent to their marriage.

Meanwhile, Antonio and Sebastian, in another part of the island, were plotting the murder of Alonso, the King of Naples. They had assumed Ferdinand to be dead, and felt that Sebastian would succeed to the throne upon Alonso's death. They intended to carry

out their wicked plan while
their victim was asleep, but
Ariel woke him in good time.

Ariel was up to his usual
tricks. He set before them a
delicious banquet, and then,
just as they were about to eat,
appeared before them in the
shape of a harpy – a voracious

monster with wings – and the feast vanished. Then, to their utter amazement, the harpy spoke to them, reminding them of their cruelty in driving Prospero from his dukedom, and leaving him and his infant daughter to perish at sea, saying that for this reason they would suffer.

The King
of Naples and
Antonio repented of
the injustice they had
done to Prospero, and Ariel told
his master he was certain their
penitence was sincere.

"Then bring them here,
Ariel," said Prospero.

Ariel soon returned with the king, his brother Sebastian, Antonio and old Gonzalo who had followed him, intrigued by the wild music he had played to draw them to his master's presence. No one except Gonzalo could recognise Prospero.

Antonio, in tears and with words of sorrow and true repentance, implored his brother for forgiveness, and the king expressed his sincere remorse for having assisted him in deposing his brother. Prospero forgave them.

Once they had promised to restore his dukedom, Prospero said to the King of Naples, "I have a gift for you, too." Prospero drew back a curtain

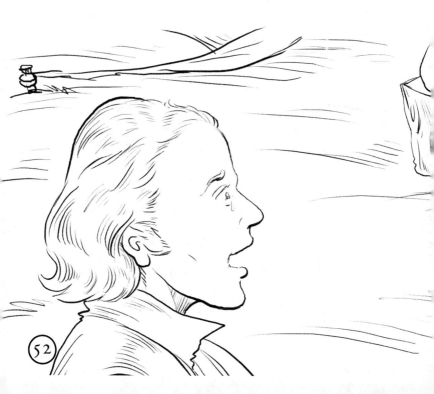

and showed him Ferdinand and
Miranda playing chess. Alonso
and his son were overjoyed to
greet each other again, for they
had each thought the other
had drowned in the storm.

The King of Naples was almost as astonished by the beauty and grace of the young Miranda as his son had been. "Who is this maid?" he asked. "She seems to be the goddess who has brought us together."

"No, sir," answered Ferdinand, amused to find that his father had made the same mistake as he had when he first saw Miranda. "She is a mortal, the daughter of Prospero, the real Duke of Milan.

I had heard much about him, but never seen him until now; I have received new life from him. And he has become a second father to me, giving me this dear lady."

"Then I must ask for her forgiveness, too," said the king. "No more of that," said

Prospero. "Let us not remember our past troubles, since they have ended so happily." And then he embraced his brother, assuring him of his forgiveness.

Prospero then told them that their ship was safe in the harbour, the sailors all on-board,

and that he and his daughter
would accompany them home
the next morning. "In the
meantime," he said, "enjoy as much
refreshment as you want; and for
your evening's entertainment, I
will tell you the story of my life
from the day I arrived on this

desert island." He then called
for Caliban to prepare some
food, and set the cave in order.

All were astonished at
the uncouth form and savage
appearance of this ugly monster,
who was the only attendant

Prospero had to wait upon him.
So all ended happily. The next
day they set sail for Naples, where
Ferdinand and Miranda were
to be married. Ariel gave them
calm seas and auspicious gales.

Prospero, after many years of absence, went back to his own dukedom, where he was welcomed with great joy by his faithful subjects. He stopped practising the art of magic and his life was happy, not only because he had found his own dukedom again, but because when his bitterest foes who had done him wrong lay at his mercy, he took no vengeance on them but nobly forgave them.

As for Ariel, Prospero set him free so that he could wander where

he wished and sing with a
light heart his sweet song.

"Where the bee sucks, there suck I:
In a cowslip's bell I lie;
There I couch when owls do cry.
On the bat's back I do fly
After summer, merrily:
Merrily, merrily, shall I live now,
Under the blossom that
hangs on the bough."